W9-CLD-363

THE
RORY STORY

BILL BINZEN

DOUBLEDAY & COMPANY, INC.
GARDEN CITY, NEW YORK

For Rory's friends
Susanna, Timothy, and *Nathaniel*

Library of Congress Cataloging in Publication Data

Binzen, Bill.
    The Rory story.

    SUMMARY: A puppy describes his daily activities.
    [1. Dogs—Fiction]   I. Title
PZ7.B51186Rr   [E]
ISBN 0-385-08752-7
ISBN 0-385-09332-2 (lib. bdg.)
Library of Congress Catalog Card Number 73-9011

U. S.   1919665

Hello. My name is Rory.
I'm just a little puppy. But
I've got big feet. That
means I'll be a big dog
someday. You'll see.

They call me Rory Underfoot. But I don't know why. There must be a reason!

I love to chew on things. Sometimes that gets me into trouble.

I often wish I had longer legs. Then I'd never lose
a race.

Running is fun. But it sure wears me out.

When I'm indoors, I want to be outdoors. When I'm outdoors, I want to be indoors. Why is that?

What's going on here? I always thought clothes were for people.

Sometimes they take me for a ride in their bus. But I'd rather walk.

But I don't like to walk on the end of a leash. Who would?

I know that dogs are supposed to catch rabbits.
So I will.

I'm good at catching kids too. But sometimes they get away.

I love playing in the woods. But I don't want to be
an Indian. I just want to be a dog.

Now this is very strange!
I thought water was to
drink.

I love to roughhouse with my friend Huck. But
I wish I wasn't ticklish.

I don't need boots. My
feet are waterproof.

I hope they come back soon. I want to go for a ride.

Hey, what are *they* doing in the lake? I thought birds lived in the sky.

Hot dog! Those birds really taught me something.

This is cool. I could stay out here forever.

I'll be glad when he learns to swim. Then we can really splash about.

At last I can grab him by the seat of his pants. He must be getting smaller.

This is *supposed* to be my house. But sometimes I wonder.

Now they've really gone too far. That's *my* stick.

If birds can swim, then I can fly. Watch me try it!

Too bad I landed on that sharp rock. Now every-
one is sure to call me Rory Sorefoot.

Maybe he'll give me one. I think a cookie would
help me feel better.

How things change. Last week, I came here for a
shower bath. Now look what's happened.

Would you believe it? This stuff just fell out of the sky.

What does he think I am? A horse? Well, I'll fool
him. I'll pull him over a bump!

Now that I'm a big dog, I guess anything goes.
But do you know what? I like it this way!